ROOTIE KAZOO
And The Final Pitch

Story by Jim Hardiman M.D.
Pictures by Randy Jennings

Rootie Kazoo loved baseball
Ever since he was small.
He slept with a bat,
Always wore a red hat,
And practiced his slide in the hall.

He spent many hours just throwing
Faster and faster while growing
Till dishes would rattle and tumble,
Causing his father to grumble.
No one knew how far he'd be going.

Rootie lived in a town called Okee
On a farm with a mulberry tree
Where he notched out the score
To a fantasy roar
And imaginary batters – strike three!

One day a man paid him a visit.
Rootie's father asked him, "What is it?"
"I heard of your son, brought my new radar gun.
Can I please just clock one?"
Said the man with the new-fangled widget.

Ready was Rootie; he reeled back to fire
With a heart full of hope and a burning desire.
The ball shot like a bolt
With the speed of a colt.
"How fast was that?" his father had to inquire.

The stunned recruiter spun,
Rubbed his eyes, checked his gun.
He said, "Rootie, you're number one.
"You could never be outdone.
I'm signing you on as a Fenokee, son."

The Fenokees played in the town of Okee.
Fans of all ages would flock to see
Baseball at its very best
From north, south, east and west
And the rookie pitcher called Rootie.

Rootie grew in favor and fame,
For he could pitch like a shooting flame,
Putting would-be hitters to shame.
His speedy pitching then ruled the game
While Fenokee fans chanted his name.

The Fenokees with Rootie kept winning
As he pitched zero scores for each inning.
His team rose to the top.
When would all this stop,
Or was this only the beginning?

Then came the big day;
The Mutzy Klutz came to play.
They were rightful champs, as people say.
Captain T-bone Tut led their way,
Dressed in blue and visitor's gray.

Tut was their star clean-up hitter.
He made pitchers sweat and their knees jitter.
When he smacked the ball it would twitter,
Lighting up the night like a meteor's glitter.
He'd turn a fierce opponent into a quitter.

Rounding the bases, Tut would trot
And ask Rootie's team, "Did you see that shot?"
They'd hide their heads as if they'd not.
They wished T-bone Tut would get off the lot
And stop strutting around like he was hot.

The time had come for the two teams meeting.
Fenokee fans watched in overflow seating.
Klutz's Tut was bragging,
Saying Rootie's team was lagging
And that they would soon take a beating.

Well, the game was a real nail-biter.
The score couldn't get any tighter.
Next came boos with the score tied at two.
As Tut approached the plate facing Rootie Kazoo,
Both were determined to be the best fighter.

Rootie wound up and threw the first pitch.
Tut swung and missed, making a ditch.
An umpire, on cue,
Yelled loudly, "Strike two!"
Before the next pitch, Tut started to twitch.

Tut was ready; he'd seen this fastball before.
He pounded the ball and broke the tied score.
When Tut rounded third,
His taunts could be heard,
And Rootie's heart sank right to the floor.

Rootie was saddened, the Okees were defeated.
Everyone left, but Rootie stayed seated.
He felt a tap on his shoulder and found he was greeted
By his father, who sat down and pleaded,
"You know a new pitch is going to be needed."

"Your fastball, it sizzles, but it's always the same.
Keeping hitters guessing is the name of the game.
I'll teach you to throw
A floater that's slow.
Keeping batters off-guard is your aim."

The Klutzes and Fenokees battled down to the wire.
Winning the trophy was both teams' desire.
With all of their eyes
Focused on the grand prize,
The teams and their fans were on fire.

The game was a doozy; the tension was absurd.
The Okees were one run ahead with a man on third.
No one could determine
A game that had fans squirmin'.
When Tut went to bat, only silence could be heard.

They were now in the ninth; Tut strutted to the box.
He had the arms of a boxer and the shoulders of an ox.
He'd been to bat twice and hit two home run knocks.
Rootie threw two pitches and blew off his socks,
And then came the time for a clever old fox.

Rootie's fans were hoping for a reason to rejoice.
He knew the time had come to make a big choice.
Tut kicked up some dirt in utter defiance.
The crowd was frozen in a deafening silence,
When from out of the stillness there blurted forth one voice.

"Now's a good time," Rootie heard the voice relate.
As Tut stared him down, Rootie set the bait.
Ready to determine T-bone Tut's fate,
Rootie sent the ball spinning toward the plate.
Tut took a swing, but he needed to wait.

Tut's bat swung quickly across the plate.
He tried to hold up, but it was a little too late.
T-bone Tut let out a loud cry
As the ball slowly floated by,
And his swing made a breeze like an old rusty gate.

"STRIKE THREE!!" screeched the umpire, "The batter is OUT!"
Fans placed Rootie on their shoulders, and they carried him about.
Even as his fans continued to rejoice,
He could hear above the crowd a familiar voice:
"Rootie, my son, I never had a doubt!"

ISBN 1-4276-1201-3

Dedicated to Luke, my son, my friend
and my favorite baseball player.
And to Donna Tabor and her projects
to help children in Nicaragua.